MR. BOUNCE

by Roger Hargreaves

Mr Bounce was very small and like a rubber ball.

He just couldn't keep himself on the ground!

He bounced all over the place!

And, as you can imagine, that made things rather difficult.

Last week, for instance, Mr Bounce was out walking when he came to a farm.

He climbed over the farm gate, and you can guess what happened next, can't you?

He jumped down from the gate, and . . .

. . . bounced right into the duckpond!

BOUNCE went Mr Bounce.

SPLASH went Mr Bounce.

"QUACK," went the ducks.

The other morning, for instance, Mr Bounce was in bed.

He woke up, and jumped out of bed, and you can guess what happened next, can't you?

He bounced right out of his bedroom door and all the way downstairs.

Bouncebouncebouncebounce!

That happens quite often, which probably explains why Mr Bounce leaves his bedroom door open every night!

After he had picked himself up Mr Bounce went inside his house and sat down to think.

BOUNCE.

Mr Bounce bounced off the chair and banged his head on the ceiling.

BANG went Mr Bounce's head on the ceiling.

"OUCH!" said Mr Bounce.

"This is ridiculous," Mr Bounce thought to himself, rubbing his head. "I must do something to stop all this bouncing about."

He thought and thought.

"I know," he thought. "I'll go and see the doctor!"

So, after breakfast, Mr Bounce set off to the nearest town to see the doctor.

He was passing a tennis court when he tripped over a pebble.

BOUNCE he bounced.

And he bounced right on to the court where two children were playing tennis, and you can guess what happened next, can't you?

The children didn't realise that Mr Bounce wasn't a tennis ball, and started hitting him with their tennis racquets backwards and forwards over the net.

BOUNCE!

"OOO!"

BOUNCE!

"OW!"

BOUNCE!

"OUCH!"

Poor Mr Bounce.

Eventually, one of the children hit Mr Bounce so hard he bounced right out of the tennis court.

Mr Bounce bounced off down the road towards the town.

"Oh dear," he said, feeling very sorry for himself. "I've been bounced black and blue!"

A bus was coming down the road, and Mr Bounce decided that the safest place for him to be would be to be on it.

He got on and sat down, still feeling more than a little sorry for himself.

The bus drove into town.

The bus stopped right outside the doctor's.

Mr Bounce stepped down from the bus.

And you can guess what happened next, can't you?

He didn't step down on to the pavement outside the doctor's. Oh no, not Mr Bounce!

He stepped off the bus, and on to the pavement, and bounced, in through the doctor's window!

Dr Makeyouwell was sitting at his desk, enjoying his mid-morning cup of coffee.

Mr Bounce sailed through the open window, and landed . . .

Well, you can guess where he landed, can't you?

That's right!

SPLASH went the coffee.

"OUCH!" squeaked Mr Bounce. The coffee was rather hot.

"Good heavens," exclaimed Dr Makeyouwell.

After the doctor had fished Mr Bounce out of his coffee, and sat him on some blotting paper to dry out, he listened to what Mr Bounce had to tell him.

"So you see," said Mr Bounce finally, "you must give me something to stop me bouncing about all over the place quite so much."

"Hmmm," pondered the doctor.

After some thought Dr Makeyouwell went to his medicine cabinet and took out a pair of tiny red boots.

"This should do the trick," he told Mr Bounce. "Heavy boots! That should stop the bouncing!"

"Oh, thank you, Dr Makeyouwell," said Mr Bounce and walked home wearing his red boots.

Not bounced!

Walked!

That night Mr Bounce went to bed wearing his heavy boots.

And then he went to sleep.

The following morning, he woke up and yawned and stretched, and bounced out of bed.

And can you guess what happened next?

No, he didn't bounce down the stairs.

He went straight through the bedroom floorboards,

and finished up in the kitchen!

Fantastic offers for Mr. Men fans!

Collect all your Mr. Men or Little Miss books in these superb durable collectors' cases!
Only £5.99 inc. postage and packing, these wipe-clean, hard-wearing cases will give all your Mr. Men or Little Miss books a beautiful new home!

Keep track of your collection with this giant-sized double-sided Mr. Men and Little Miss Collectors' poster.
Collect 6 tokens and we will send you a brilliant giant-sized double-sided collectors' poster! Simply tape a £1 coin to cover postage and packing in the space provided and fill out the form overleaf.

STICK £1 COIN HERE
(for poster only)

Only need a few Mr. Men or Little Miss to complete your set? You can order any of the titles on the back of the books from our Mr. Men order line on 0870 787 1724. Orders should be delivered between 5 and 7 working days.

─────── **TO BE COMPLETED BY AN ADULT** ───────

To apply for any of these great offers, ask an adult to complete the details below and send this whole page with the appropriate payment and tokens, to: MR. MEN CLASSIC OFFER, PO BOX 715, HORSHAM RH12 5WG

☐ Please send me a giant-sized double-sided collectors' poster.
AND ☐ I enclose 6 tokens and have taped a £1 coin to the other side of this page.

☐ Please send me ☐ Mr. Men Library case(s) and/or ☐ Little Miss library case(s) at £5.99 each inc P&P

☐ I enclose a cheque/postal order payable to Egmont UK Limited for £................................

OR ☐ Please debit my MasterCard / Visa / Maestro / Delta account (delete as appropriate) for £................................

Card no. ☐☐☐☐☐☐☐☐☐☐☐☐☐☐☐☐☐☐☐☐ Security code ☐☐☐

Issue no. (if available) ☐ Start Date ☐☐/☐☐/☐☐ Expiry Date ☐☐/☐☐/☐☐

Fan's name: .... Date of birth: ....

Address: ....

....

Postcode: ....

Name of parent / guardian: ....

Email for parent / guardian: ....

Signature of parent / guardian: ....

Please allow 28 days for delivery. Offer is only available while stocks last. We reserve the right to change the terms of this offer at any time and we offer a 14 day money back guarantee. This does not affect your statutory rights. Offers apply to UK only.

☐ We may occasionally wish to send you information about other Egmont children's books.
If you would rather we didn't, please tick this box.

Ref: MRM 001